To Matil

Mark

Cougar Adventurers Edition

This Tomser Cat Book
Belongs To:

_____

_____

See if you can spot Tomser Cat
hiding somewhere in the pages of this book!

To Seren,
Our own little Polly!
Thanks for your Bubbly inspiration!
With Love, Dad & Mum x x

First published in 2014 by Tomser Cat Books

This Edition published in 2019 by Tomser Cat Books
Ty Mawr House
Bryn Henwysg
Troedrhiw-Trwyn
Pontypridd CF37 2SE

www.tomsercat.com

A CIP catalogue record for this book is available from the British
Library

ISBN: 978-1-912169-06-1

Printed in Great Britain

Polly's Magic Bubbles
and the Quest for Dizzelwood

Mark Dorey

illustrated by Liz Dorey

Cougar Adventurers Edition

Tomser Cat Books

Other brilliant books by Mark & Liz Dorey

Cougars (for adventurers 7 to 11)

Polly's Magic Bubbles – Revenge of the Spiders

The Mystery of the Un-Snowy Mountain
and the
Great Deep Sleep Miscalculation

Big Cats (young adults and older adventurers too)

The Extraordinary Happenings of Peter Oddfellow:
The Old Umbrella

The Green Eyes of Darkness by Michael C Thomas

Into The Shattered Dark by Michael C Thomas

In The Coldest Dark by Michael C Thomas

Mousers (picture books for our youngest readers)

Can We Walk to the Moon?

How High Do Trees Grow?

The Story of How God Un-Invisibled Himself

Help! I'm Lost Property!

Bobcats (Illustrated Chapter Books for First readers)

Midge - Prince of the Giants

Polly's Magic Bubbles
and the Quest for Dizzelwood

Chapter One

TOO LATE!

"Sorry," said the man peering into his empty suitcase. "They're all gone."

"All gone?" Polly gaped in disbelief. "But you had three left; a blue one, a green one and a—"

The Bubble gun seller shrugged, his grubby T-shirt failing miserably to cover his bulging stomach. "Sold the last one a few minutes ago."

"But I wasn't that long, and you promised!" Polly gave him her best annoyed stare, her £2.50 weighing heavily in her hand.

The man scratched the patchy clumps of hair stuck to his chin like bits of dirty cotton wool, clearly not used to being stared at by disappointed and very annoyed eight-year-olds. "Sorry," he said sheepishly.

"You snooze, you lose."

Polly definitely hadn't snoozed, so she didn't know how she could have lost anything, but lost she had. Tears started to well up in her eyes.

"Look, come back next week," said the man, hastily packing away his empty case before shuffling off.

The park was filled with kids, laughing and playing with bubbles floating everywhere, some of them most probably coming from a bubble gun that should have belonged to Polly.

She stared down at her unspent £2.50 in despair.

"Excuse me…" said a voice.

Polly nearly jumped out of her skin. A wiry old man wearing an ill-fitting suit stood behind her.

"You like them, don't you?" The old man bent close, his crooked, tall green hat teetering above blue eyes that sparkled and danced. A stale smell wafted from his crumpled moss-brown suit, much too close to Polly's crinkling nose. "The bubbles," he said. "I saw you watching the bubbles."

Polly didn't know what to do – she knew that she shouldn't speak to strangers. She looked around to see if she could see her parents or the park keeper, but there was no one around, so she just nodded.

The old man smiled a surprisingly dazzling smile. "Well, today is your lucky day!"

Polly wasn't sure whether to make a run for it. "Sorry, but I really have to go…"

"Oh no, no, no, there's no need to go – today is your lucky day!" his big beaming smile and twinkling eyes somehow made him look a lot younger.

"Sorry mister, you must be mistak—"

"I've got some bubbles, bigger and better than any bubble gun!" Then he bent in very close, his wrinkly face filling Polly's vision with a sudden deadly seriousness. "How much money do you have?"

Transfixed and unable to move, Polly opened her hand as a fresh waft of his stale pongy-ness slapped her in the face and filled her nostrils.

"Mmmm…" the man examined the £2.50 in her hand carefully. "I'm not sure whether that's going to be enough." He glanced over his shoulder, looking this way and that, before turning his attention back to Polly. "But then again," his eyes twinkled mischievously, "I think I can trust you." Another dazzling smile flashed across his face before once again it turned really serious; the most serious looking face that Polly had ever seen as he bent in even closer. "I can trust you, can't I?"

Not sure of what else to do, Polly nodded dumbly.

The old man rummaged inside his crumpled jacket, searching with wiry fingers.

Feeling increasingly nervous and desperate to leave, Polly blurted out. "I have to go, my parents will—"

"Ah-Ha! Here it is!" The old man waved his hand in the air with a flourish, as if conducting an invisible band.

Polly turned to walk away. "I have to go!"

"Don't you want to see?" The old man was somehow in front of her, his hand outstretched.

"Bubbles," he said, his blue eyes sparkling.

There in his wrinkled hand was a tiny green bottle, crowned with a gold top that shone like the sun – like a normal bottle of bubbles but a lot prettier and a lot, lot smaller.

Polly dodged past his hand. "I really have to go..."

"Magic bubbles!" said the old man triumphantly, his eyebrows coming alive.

Polly stopped dead in her tracks.

Magic bubbles!

"Yes, indeed!" said the old man reading her thoughts, his head bobbing up and down on an invisible spring.

Polly turned for a closer look.

The old man snatched his hand away. "Ah, ah, ah... money first."

There can't be many bubbles in there...

"Oh, I promise you, little one, there's all the bubbles you'll ever need right inside!" The old man's eyebrows danced up and down like fluffy caterpillars.

Maybe, thought Polly, *but they'd be too tiny to see.*

"These bubbles are much bigger than you could possibly imagine, and each and every one jam-packed-filled with adventures!" The old man bent in again, so close that their noses were almost touching, and in a loud whisper added. "Bigger and better than any bubble gun!"

Polly thought for a moment. "How much?"

The old man scratched his chin thoughtfully. "Well, normally a lot more than what you have there, but I would hate for you to be disappointed twice in one day."

Polly looked around again to see if she could see her parents. "I don't know – I was supposed to get a bubble gun... Sorry to waste your time, but I really have to go..." She turned back to face the old man, but he had vanished into thin air!

How strange!

Polly breathed a sigh of relief. The old man was a bit

creepy, but at least he was gone now.

Magic bubbles, what nonsense!

Polly went to put her money back in her pocket, but her money was gone! There in her hand was the tiny green bottle with a top that shone like the sun. But that was not all. The bottle was resting on a crumpled piece of yellowed paper. Polly unravelled the paper, which was weathered and worn like old parchment.

The paper was blank.

She was about to crumple it up and put it in her pocket to throw away later, when to her amazement some writing began to appear on it:

Thank you for purchasing your Magic Bubbles!
Twelve blows – but not too hard!
Only twelve and no more.
Use your last Bubbles very carefully!
Refunds definitely not available.

Before Polly could examine the paper and its peculiar message any further, a sudden gust of wind blew the parchment out of her hand, where it promptly vanished in a puff of smoke!

Chapter Two

MAGIC BUBBLES

Polly stared at the shiny green bottle in her hand.

What a waste of £2.50!

Carefully unscrewing the gold top, she took out the blower. The stick was as thin as a needle, all jagged with a tiny hole hardly big enough to see through, let alone blow a bubble!

'Much bigger than you could ever imagine!
Bigger and better than any bubble gun!'

The old man's voice stirred on the breeze, although he was nowhere to be seen.

Polly held the blower up for a closer look. A sudden gust of wind caused the teeny-tiny amount of soapy liquid to form a bubble, which grew Bigger...

and BIGGER...

and BIGGER...

The bubble was bigger than the size of her head!

Polly stared, open mouthed as the bubble detached itself and started to bounce over the grass like a large see-through football.

With each bounce, it picked up flowers and blades of grass as if plucking them with an invisible hand. Quickly screwing the top back on the tiny container, Polly gave chase.

Closer and closer and closer, the bubble now almost in reach...

Another gust of wind launched the bubble skywards, up and over the trees until it vanished from view.

'Eleven bubbles left,' said the old man's voice, although he was still nowhere to be seen.

Polly sighed as she gazed at the tiny bottle in her hand.

Maybe they were magic bubbles after all...

'Oh yes, they are! They are indeed, but there's only eleven left.'

Polly looked all around. There was no sign of him anywhere.

Perhaps the old man was spying on her from somewhere in the trees?

Polly stared at the bottle again. This needed a little more investigating.

"POLLYANNA!"

Polly nearly jumped out of her skin.

"What *are* you doing?" barked her Mum, marching briskly towards her.

Polly was in **BIG TROUBLE** – Mum had used Polly's full name.

"Sorry, Mum. I was... er... chasing bubbles."

"Well, would you mind chasing them where I can see you? Come on, it looks like it's going to rain."

Polly sighed. *Why did it always rain on school holidays?*

They re-joined her Dad and two brothers, Jake and Joshy. Jake, her older brother by four years always had his nose in some magazine or other; Joshy, having just turned two was relishing his new found walking and exploring ability and getting into just about anything and everything. Dad, as always, was dressed in old fashioned clothes (at least thirty years too old for him), puffing on his permanently unlit pipe.

As they walked back home, Polly's mind tumbled over and over with thoughts of magic bubbles and her curious encounter with the strange old man.

The rain came and went in a quick shower, soon rushing away eager to catch anyone else still lingering about outdoors. Not long after Polly got home, there was a knock on the door.

It was Marcia, Polly's best friend. Completely unalike, Polly's long, straw red hair and freckly skin contrasted sharply with Marcia's near perfect complexion, crowned with the blondest, curliest hair of anyone she knew.

Marcia lived two doors away and would quite often pop around without warning. Polly didn't mind, she always enjoyed Marcia's unexpected visits. Now she could finally tell someone about her secret and very unintentional purchase!

Polly ushered Marcia quickly upstairs and told her the story of the strange old man and the magic bubbles.

Marcia's eyes grew as big as saucers. "Let me see, let me see!"

Polly reached into her pocket. It was empty! She searched with desperate fingers inside her pocket.

ARRGHH! A HOLE!

Polly scoured her bedroom floor, then down the stairs, through the dining room, desperately retracing her steps, shadowed by a twittering Marcia.

The magic bubbles were gone. Trudging back to her bedroom, a gloomy Polly flumped onto her bed.

"Have you tried looking in your other pocket?" suggested Marcia.

"No!" snapped Polly, "I always keep things in my right pocket."

"Oh," shrugged Marcia.

Polly delved her hand into her left pocket. Her fingers touched something. Pulling out the something, Polly stared in disbelief at the tiny bottle in her hand.

"You found it!" Marcia was jumping up and down with excitement, her blond woolly hair like a leaping springtime lamb.

"But I never put things in my left pocket."

"Well, you did this time," said Marcia. "Come on, let's see your magic bubbles!"

Polly took out the blower but before she could do anything, Marcia snatched it, blowing through the tiny hole filled with soapy liquid.

A large bubble quickly formed, much to the disbelieving gasps of the two children standing in wide-eyed amazement.

Bigger...

and BIGGER...

and BIGGER...

The bubble floated in the air before bobbing onto her bed and swallowing up Alfie, Polly's treasured teddy.

"Alfie's floating in the bubble!" exclaimed Marcia.

The bubble continued hovering around Polly's bedroom, both girls ducking out of the way as it floated towards the wall. When it got to the wall, instead of popping, it simply floated straight through, both Alfie and the bubble vanishing from sight.

"He's gone through the wall!" screamed Marcia as both girls rushed to the window to see the large bubble and the trapped Alfie floating off into the distance. The further away it got, the more it looked like Alfie was flying all by himself.

"He's floating over the rooftops!" shrieked Marcia, her excitement rising by the second.

'Ten bubbles left,' said the old man's voice.

"Did you hear that?" asked Polly.

"Hear what?"

"Nothing," sighed Polly.

Marcia's eyes were wide with excitement.

"Let's try another one!" she squeaked.

Polly was unsure. "I don't know..."

"Oh, come on! Just one more."

"There's only ten left."

"*PLEEEASE!*" pleaded Marcia, with big puppy-dog eyes.

"Okay, but I'm doing it," insisted Polly.

Marcia started to protest.

"Marcia, they're my bubbles!" Polly dabbed the blower back into the bottle, having to turn her back on her friend to stop her from interfering. Polly took a deep breath and began to blow, the bubble getting Bigger... and BIGGER...

and BIGGER...
until it almost filled the room!

"Let's get inside!" Marcia rushed forward and was inside the bubble before Polly could stop her. The giant bubble took Marcia's weight easily as it floated around her bedroom.

"Woooo!" shouted Marcia excitedly. "Look at me! Look at me! I'm flying!"

Polly couldn't look for long because the giant bubble was already disappearing through her bedroom wall. Polly rushed to the window as the giant bubble bobbed over the rooftops with Marcia giggling wildly.

"Look at me, I'm flying, I'm flying, I'm flying!"

There was only one thing left to do.

Polly dabbed the blower and blew another large bubble. Quickly stashing it safely in her left pocket, she clambered through the bubble wall, and just as her best friend had done moments before, she started floating around the room.

'Eight bubbles left.'

The old man's voice echoed through the bubble as Polly vanished through the brickwork and drifted into the outside world.

Chapter Three

Over the Rooftops

Soon Polly was floating over the rooftops. Marcia was still in sight, but only just.

Polly had to go faster, *but how*?

Although the bubble seemed strong enough, she didn't want to do anything that might make it suddenly go

Think, Polly. Think!

Taking a deep breath, Polly began to walk along the inside of the bubble. Slowly, the bubble began to rotate. Quickening her stride, the bubble spun ever faster. With Polly now running as fast as she could, the bubble began to gain on Marcia in the distance.

It was working!

A few exhausting minutes later, a breathless Polly finally caught up, with the two bubbles now floating side by side.

"Isn't this amazing?" squealed Marcia.

Amazing or not, they had no idea where they were heading, or perhaps more importantly, how they were ever going to get back. The two magical bubbles bobbed and skimmed above the rooftops, narrowly missing chimney pots and spiky-balloon-popping TV aerials.

Much to Polly's relief, both bubbles started to climb rapidly, although Marcia was far too excited to care.

The houses below grew smaller and smaller as the two transparent spheres floated ever higher. It was really weird seeing everything from so high up: cars, vans, lorries and buses streamed through thick-stringed roads snaking between houses, shops and other buildings.

Higher and higher they floated, the entire village laid out like a wonderful carpet. The surrounding fields were dappled with speckles of sheepy-white and slightly larger black-cow-blobs.

Polly's attention turned to a faint whirring sound on the air. The noise grew **louder** and **LOUDER**. A large dark brown humming bird was flying towards them at an impossible speed.

Marcia's excitement reached new levels. "Oooh, look, it's a birdie. Hello, Mr Bird!"

Polly wasn't so sure. "Marcia, I don't think..."

As the bird closed in, Marcia's excitement began to turn to panic. "Shoo, birdie! Shoo!"

The bird hovered all around the bubbles, its wings a blur of motion as it inspected the floating girls with cold unblinking eyes. Then, landing atop Marcia's bubble, it regarded her intently. Its wings were a rusty colour, dry and crinkly, tinted dark red at the edges, almost like autumn leaves. Its beak was sharp like a tapered arrow, although a bit crooked, and it had a blaze of bright orangey-red on its breast. It was the strangest bird that either of them had ever seen.

"*SHOO! SHOO!* Don't you dare peck my bubble! Don't you dare! *SHOO! SHOO!*"

"Marcia, I don't think he understands."

The strange bird continued to examine the springy surface, its head moving left and right, its sharp beak edging ever nearer to the outside of Marcia's bubble.

"*PLEEEASE*, Mr Bird, please go away!" begged Marcia.

Much to Marcia's relief and Polly's horror, the bird hovered across to Polly's bubble.

It stared at her as if searching for something. Polly had a sinking feeling in the bottom of her stomach.

Polly reached into her pocket to unscrew the tiny blower.

The bird's head dropped.

The girls screamed.

Polly tumbled helplessly groundwards as Marcia floated away, closely pursued by the bird assassin in a blurring whirr of wings.

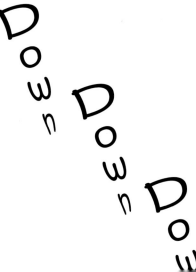

Polly tumbling over... and over... and over... and over

Blue became green

then green became blue

as sky became land

and land became sky.

The wind whistling by as Polly fell, her arms flailing.

"HEEELLLLPPP!"

As Polly's arms flapped frantically, a bubble began to form in the blower, growing Bigger...

and BIGGER...

and **BIGGER...**

a springy bubbly mattress floating underneath Polly. No longer in freefall, she floated up again, sprawled on the outside of the giant magic bubble.

Polly breathed a sigh of relief as a loud Marcia scream split the air.

The nasty bird had

POPPED

Marcia's bubble!

Down and down Marcia plunged, her hair a buffeting frizzy cloud as Polly continued to rise.

There wouldn't be much time...

Polly reached out, grabbing Marcia as she tumbled past, their combined weight pulling them safely inside her bubble, which luckily remained intact.

They were safe.

Another shriek split the air. The bird was coming back!

Polly had an idea!

Pushing hard, she forced her head through the bubble, Polly yelled at the top of her voice. "Come on! Come on! Try and pop this bubble!"

Marcia frantically tugged on Polly's arm. *"Polly, what are you doing?"*

Polly ignored her as she continued taunting the rapidly approaching bird.

Closer...

Closer...

Closer...

The bird now almost on top of them, Marcia closed her eyes and screamed. Polly blew another bubble, this one aimed at their winged pursuer. Before the bird could change course, it became trapped inside the other bubble, which now floated up and away from the two girls, the bird pecking furiously at the inside trying to break its way out, but without success.

"The bubbles are stronger on the inside," explained Polly as Marcia stared at her in disbelief.

'Six bubbles left ...' echoed a familiar voice.

"I know, I know!" snapped Polly, beginning to feel more than a little fed up.

"What's that?" asked Marcia.

"Nothing," said Polly, gritting her teeth. "Now please sit still before this one pops too!"

Chapter Four

RAINBOW RIDE

The afternoon sun rose high on a canvas of blue sky as the girls floated ever higher.

"I wonder where we're going?" asked Marcia.

"I don't know," snapped Polly, still feeling a bit cross.

Polly wasn't sure why she was cross, she just was. Somehow, the strange old man who sold her the bubbles was still watching them.

But how could that be?

Now, she wasn't even sure where they were going. The only sure thing that Polly could be sure of was that she was in **BIG TROUBLE!**

How were they ever going to get back home?

Even if they did get back home, she'd still be in

BIG TROUBLE!

Marcia could never, ever keep a secret. Polly remembered the time when—

"Look, a rainbow!" Marcia pointed towards a mass of colour arcing across the sky. "We're heading towards a rainbow!"

The bubble was picking up speed as if the rainbow were a giant bubble magnet. Soon they were floating inside the vibrant colours of the rainbow itself. It was the most wonderful thing ever, the bubble coming alive with colour, its shiny see-through surface reflecting thousands of tiny rainbows everywhere.

Marcia giggled excitedly, pointing at this colour and that colour and saying how wonderful this was, and how wonderful that was.

Suddenly, everything stopped – or not exactly stopped, Marcia's voice simply faded, as if someone had turned her volume right down to zero.

A strange song filled the inside of the bubble:

*You have a song that only you can sing
A song that breathes life into everything'*

The song floated on the air like the faintest musical breeze.

Was it Polly's imagination?

She glanced across to Marcia, who was still pointing at this and that, talking excitedly but with no sound whatsoever.

You have a song that only you can sing
A song that breathes life into everything'

Polly felt another presence.

Someone else.

She turned slowly, hardly daring to look. There was a face – a face reflected in the surface of the bubble.

Maybe it was a trick of the light?

No. It was definitely a face. A face looking directly at her. The face smiled. She'd seen that face somewhere before...

"W-W-Who are you?"

'I'm part of the Magic.'

"What do you want? Why has everything gone quiet? What's happened to Marcia?"

'Listen carefully, there is very little time. Everything will soon go back to as it was. I want you to remember, remember your song.'

"What song? What are you talking about?"

'You have a song that only you can sing A song that breathes life into everything'

"But I don't have a song—"

'The time will come.'

"What time? Please, you don't understand, I don't-"

'Remember...'

The face started to fade.

"Wait, don't go! You need to tell me. You must—"

The face was almost gone, it's voice now a long, lingering whisper.

'Remember...'

A song exploded the silence.

"SOOME-WHEEERE OVER THE RAIN-BOW, WAY UP HIGH!"

Marcia's off-key singing shook and rattled the colours all around them.

Polly's mood started to lift, her cross thoughts of

BIG TROUBLE no longer seeming to matter.

A fleeting thought shot across the back of her mind. Something she couldn't quite remember...

But one thing Polly knew for sure: she was floating inside a rainbow with her best friend and now all she wanted to do was sing!

Taking Marcia by the hand, the two girls danced and sang and laughed in the waterfalls of colour washing over them.

"Soome-wheeere over the rain-bow, way up high!"

Time passed, although neither of them had any idea how much, the two girls just sitting together happily as the magic bubble continued its journey through the colours of the rainbow.

It was Marcia who noticed it first. "I think we're going down," she said.

And so they were.

The bubble was following the arc of the rainbow back down to the ground. Far below, a dark forest awaited.

"I wonder if there's a crock of gold," said Marcia. "Mum says that at the end of every rainbow there's always a crock of gold."

As they drifted just above the treetops, both girls held each other tight, hoping they wouldn't get

by the branches as they continued their descent into a small clearing.

Chapter Five

A STICKY ENCOUNTER

The balloon popped as it touched the ground. The air felt chilly even though it was the summer holidays.

The leaves on the surrounding trees although still firmly attached were withered and brown, just like autumn. The ground was bare earth, with not a blade of grass anywhere to be seen.

The hairs rose on the back of Polly's neck.

Someone was watching them.

"**Hellooooo!**" Polly's voice echoed around the clearing, weaving in and out of the trees and coming back in a spooky echo-ey chorus of "Hello!" "Hello!" "Hello!" "Hello!" "Hello!" "Hello!" "Hello!" "Hello!" "Hello!" "Hello!" "Hello!"

Marcia clung on Polly's arm. "Maybe we should get out of here," she said.

Polly nodded, reaching for the small container in her pocket.

Something moved through the trees in the distance.

"What was that?" whispered Marcia.

"Dunno," answered Polly, not sure what to do next.

"Maybe we should—"

The something moved again, this time just off to the side. Whatever it was, it was moving quickly.

"I think you're right," said Polly. "Let's get out of here."

"Is that you?" asked a voice.

Both girls froze, Polly's heart thumping like a big bass drum and threatening to escape straight through her chest!

"Did you hear that?" whispered Marcia, pressing tight into Polly's back.

Polly nodded.

"Is that you?" asked the voice again.

"Who?" asked Polly.

"You," replied the voice.

"I – I guess so," replied Polly.

"Good," said the voice. "I thought you would never come."

"You... you knew we were coming?"

"Of course, of course!"

"But we didn't—"

"You were given the Magic, weren't you?"

Polly clasped the container tightly in her pocket. "What sort of magic?"

"The one you're holding in your hand," replied the voice simply.

"How do you...?"

"I can see it."

"But it's in my pocket."

"The Magic cannot be hidden," explained the voice. "At least, not from me."

"And... who exactly *are* you?" asked Polly, not sure if she really wanted to know.

"My name is Izz," said Izz, stepping into the clearing from nowhere.

Izz was the oddest creature Polly had ever seen, looking like an odd collection of sticks hastily thrown together into a human form. No more than three feet tall, Izz had thin twig arms and legs with knotty bits forming his clumpy body. His head was small and round with the tiniest of twigs for hair. Izz had a long, slightly crooked nose (that looked oddly familiar), and a swizzly mouth. His pea-sized eyes were friendly but unblinking.

Izz looked around. "I could have sworn there were two of you, but I don't seem to—"

"There's me as well," squeaked Marcia, hidden just behind Polly.

"Oh, I see, or rather, I don't... which reminds me."

Izz put both hands over his mouth and blew softly. A

chorus of owl hoots and birdsong filled the rusty forest air. Moments later, there was a stirring in the wood just beyond the clearing.

One of the trees was coming alive! The towering creature lumbered into the clearing, its woody form a giant nine-foot replica of Izz.

THEY WERE DONE FOR!

Polly withdrew the magic bubbles, quickly unscrewing the lid, as Marcia cowered behind.

"STOP!" yelled Izz.

Both Polly and the stick giant froze.

"No need to waste the Magic." Izz turned to face the stick giant, unimpressed and very annoyed. "Ozz, Igg, Ogg – stop that at once! Is this any way to treat our guests?"

The stick giant remained stationary, at least for a bit. Then it started to sway, before splitting into three distinct pieces, the top and middle tumbling down into three exact replicas of Izz. The tree sprites regarded Polly with unblinking eyes, looking ever so sorry.

"May I introduce my brothers, Ozz, Igg and Ogg," said Izz.

The three stick men bowed in a chorus of creaks.

Izz smiled apologetically. "Sometimes my brothers can get carried away, particularly if they think there's danger."

"That's okay," said Polly managing a smile as she screwed the top back on the tiny bottle before replacing it in her pocket. "This is my best friend, Marcia," she said, holding her hand out in friendship, "and my name's Polly."

The four tree sprites held out their hands too, but stayed put.

"Pleased to meet you," said Polly, a little awkwardly.

"Pleased to meet you," echoed the chorus of stick men.

"Me too," added Marcia weakly.

Izz smiled. "Welcome to Dizzelwood. We're so glad you're here. We were beginning to think that you'd not received the Magic."

"But—" began Polly.

Izz raised his hand. "Unfortunately, we have no time to stand around and talk. The Queen and Stick Council awaits. Come!"

Chapter Six

A MEETING WITH THE QUEEN

The stick men scampered off, the two girls following quickly through the decaying autumnal forest. The sprites moved swiftly despite their small size, often blending into the woody background as they navigated their way through the autumn foliage.

"I wonder where we're going?" panted Marcia.

"To see the Queen and the Stick Council," replied Polly breathing heavily, her eyes tracking the stick men flitting into the distance.

Just when the girls thought they could run no more, Izz, Ozz, Igg and Ogg stopped. They were in a large banked amphitheatre of trees, all wrapped with twisting vines, their high-arched roots growing out of the ground to form wooden arch caves at the base of the tree trunks. They were the weirdest trees the girls had ever seen.

The whole arena was covered by the intricate root structure of the hugest tree imaginable arching high overhead. It was almost as if the earth had been scooped out by a giant hand, revealing the secret root structure criss-crossing beneath the giant tree. Lots and lots of dark passages extended up into the inside of the enormous trunk. The whole surface of the tree was covered in speckly grey mould, and as with everywhere else in the forest, the earth was bare, with not a single blade of grass to be seen.

Izz cupped his hands and blew. A strange and beautiful hum floated through the tree roots as each of the stick brothers glanced around expectantly.

Izz blew again, then a third time.

"Do you think they're—" began Marcia in a loud whisper.

The vines on the surrounding trees began to move and detach. They fell like arrows in showers of stick rain, magically transforming into an army of stick people as they hit the ground. Whether they were male or female, it was impossible to tell. Moments later, the gathered ocean of stick people parted in a creaking *WHOOSH*, creating a pathway down the middle.

Izz stepped forward. "HER MOST ROYAL AND REGAL HIGHNESS, THE QUEEN!"

Polly and Marcia stiffened at the prospect of being presented to Stick Royalty.

Radiant in a flowing brown dress, a stunningly elegant old woman stepped through the gathering hordes, her long grey hair wound in elaborate patterns atop her head, through which a crown of simple dried flowers were interwoven.

A latticed throne was hastily shuffled into position, the Queen's gaze sweeping over her subjects as she sat. Moments later, a parade of slightly taller, more regal-looking stick men entered the arena. The Stick Council seated themselves on smaller chairs either side of their monarch.

The Queen regarded the two young girls solemnly.

"Thank you, my dears, for coming," her voice though not loud, carried an air of authority.

Polly and Marcia performed their best curtsies, Marcia's slightly wobblier.

"The forest is sick," continued the Queen. "What you see before you now is not as it once was and things are getting worse, much, much worse." The Queen lifted her head to the enormous tree arching overhead. "The Tree of Light will not last much longer, I fear."

A subdued murmur rustled throughout the gathering as the stick people nodded their unified agreement.

The Queen unexpectedly smiled. "I see you have brought the Magic."

Another wave of rustling murmurs, this time of approval.

"I have some bubbles," said Polly. "I bought them from an old man—"

"The King," stated the Queen.

"Oh no, he wasn't a King, he was an old gentleman. He gave me the bubbles and then vanished."

Marcia nodded her head in vigorous agreement like an affectionate puppy.

Another Royal smile. "That sounds like him."

"But—"

"The King has been kidnapped and the forest is under a curse."

"But, how could he— "

"The King, although weakened, is not without power, although I suspect that he used the last of it getting the Magic to you."

"But why Polly?" blurted out Marcia.

"To keep the Magic safe," replied the Queen, "from the Enemy."

"The Enemy?" asked Marcia, unable to stop herself.

"Whoever kidnapped the King," guessed Polly.

The Queen nodded.

"Oh," said Marcia.

"As to the Enemy's identity," continued the Queen, "you've already encountered him."

"We have?" bleated Marcia in astonishment. "You mean he's one of..." Marcia nodded pointedly towards Izz, Ozz, Igg and Ogg.

"No," said the Queen. "Izz and his brothers are some of my most loyal subjects."

The four stick brothers beamed with pride.

"The humming bird," said Polly, "with the leafy wings and orangey breast."

The Queen nodded. "You are quick, my dear."

Polly did her best not to blush.

"Sor-Ben-Rez can take many forms but the orange crest he cannot disguise. He used to be Head Counsel and Advisor to the King and myself, a position affording him every luxury. Yet he wanted more." The Queen trailed off, her eyes filled with sorrow. It was some time before she spoke again. "The King is being held captive." She looked directly at Polly. "We need your help."

"But what can we possibly do?" asked Polly.

"You must use the Magic. It will take you to the King."

"But—"

"You have been Chosen!" snapped the Queen, ending any further debate.

"But, what about Sorby Razz?" asked Marcia.

"Sor-Ben-Rez has great power. Fortunately, the Magic is stronger. It must be used against him, but it will take two."

"Two?" asked Polly.

"Two has great power. Only two can rescue the King and banish Sor-Ben-Rez forever. Only then can the woodland be restored."

"Yippee!" squeaked Marcia, clapping her hands. As she clapped, the light in the forest dimmed, the clapping now echoing as loud cracks of thunder.

Marcia stopped, uncertain of what she had started, but the terrible thunder continued. A dark wind howled through the amphitheatre bending the stick people like wheat in a field. The Queen yelled a command, her voice lost in the gale. The crowds of stick people fell to the ground flattened like twiggy dominoes. An orange light burst through the darkness, a blazing fireball, although there was no heat, the thunder now almost unbearable. Polly and Marcia huddled down, burying their heads under their arms. Just when Polly thought she could take no more, both dazzling light and terrible darkness were gone, along with the wind as everything returned to as it was before.

Polly unfurled her arms and looked around. Only the Queen was still standing, defiant and resolute. Polly stood up straight as Marcia staggered to her feet, looking lost and bewildered. One by one, and then in greater numbers, the stick people regained their feet.

The Queen turned her gaze to Polly. "Time is running out."

Polly's resolve hardened. "How do we use the Magic?"

The Queen smiled, a kind but weak smile. "The King entrusted it to you. It is yours to use as you see fit."

Polly's resolve faltered as a dark sinking feeling hit the bottom of her stomach.

The Queen continued. "Izz and his brothers will take you to the Tree of Darkness, but no further. Too many have already fallen asleep and been lost. All our hopes rest on you."

All eyes turned to Polly.

Polly let out a deep sigh. "I guess that's it then."

The Queen nodded. "There will be much danger, and difficult choices lay ahead, but I know that you will do the right thing. Farewell."

The Queen turned and left, followed closely by the Stick Council and the hordes of stick people until only Izz, Ozz, Igg and Ogg remained.

![stick figure]

Chapter Seven

THE TREE OF DARKNESS

Polly looked around the empty arena and then up at the huge tree towering overhead, all the while the stick brothers looking on expectantly.

"Come on," sighed Polly, "it's time to go."

"Yippee!" said Marcia.

Polly wished she felt as cheery as they followed Izz and his brothers out of the root covered arena.

As they travelled on through the forest, the air grew colder and colder. By the time they stopped, the girls' cloudy breaths hung on the frosty air, accompanied by Marcia's loud shivering noises.

Izz, Ozz, Igg and Ogg stood before a huge hollowed out tree, lying on the ground, its huge trunk stretching off into the growing gloom.

"The Tree of Darkness," said Izz gravely, his stick brothers looking equally concerned. "We can take you no further. You must go on alone."

The entrance to the hollowed trunk was covered in a sticky film shimmering with icy dew.

"Ugh!" grimaced Marcia. "Spiders!"

A loud **CRACK!** sounded from high above.

As one, the four stick brothers threw themselves at the two girls, knocking them sideways as a large branch smashed into the ground where they were standing just moments before.

Izz helped a dazed Polly back to her feet. "There is much danger. The Magic will guide you. Farewell."

Before Polly or Marcia could respond, the stick brothers had vanished.

"Look at my lovely dress," cried Marcia. "It's all crinkled and messy!"

"Come on, Marcia, it looks like it's just us two," sighed Polly.

'Two has great power.'

Polly wasn't so sure. She wasn't sure of anything anymore. Marcia pointed to Polly's pocket.

"I didn't know you had a torch."

Polly took out the magic container, the green casing and gold top shining with an eerie glow.

"It's the Magic," gasped Marcia.

Polly raked the webs clear from the lower part of the hollow tree, well over twenty feet in diameter. The broken strands clung to her fingers as a chill blast of air funnelled through the darkness. The coldness was unlike anything she'd ever felt before, a dark-edged cold, sinister and penetrating. The unrelenting gloom and stifling darkness clung to the glowing edges of the Magic, desperate to extinguish its comforting light.

Taking a deep breath, Polly stepped inside, the sound of dried sticks cracking ominously beneath each step she took. Dozens of pairs of lifeless stick eyes stared back in the eerie glow of the Magic, heads all separated from their stick bodies lying covered in a sea of cobwebs.

'Too many have already fallen asleep and been lost'

Polly shivered as the Queen's words echoed through her mind.

"What is it?" whispered Marcia.

"Nothing," said Polly. "Let's go."

"What about the spiders?"

Polly shot Marcia a stern look. "I can't do this alone! Remember what the Queen said. Now, stay close."

They trod carefully through the murky passageway, step by stick-snapping step. The further they walked, the less crunchy the covering underfoot became, until eventually, they were walking on the mossy underside of the giant hollow trunk.

"What was that?" breathed Marcia, pulling her friend to a halt.

"What?" asked Polly.

"That sound."

Polly listened, but couldn't hear anything. "It's nothing, you're most probably imagining—"

Then she heard it, faint at first but gradually getting louder.

Louder...
and
Closer...

It sounded like—

"Spiders!" shrieked Marcia. "It's a giant spider!"

There, at the edge of the Magic's eerie glow, eyes cut like black diamonds stared back at them, unblinking.

"USE THE MAGIC!" screamed Marcia.

"No!" snapped Polly. "There's only six bubbles left."

"Use them, use them!" pleaded Marcia.

"Do keep quiet!" Polly sounded like her mother. "It's not moving. Now, let me think."

This was a very brave thing for Polly to say because in truth, she didn't know what to think or what to do next. She stretched out the Magic for a closer look, even though she didn't want to see the full horror of what they were facing. The shadowy spider backed off as the light crept forward, the arachnid remaining between the darkness and the light, but not before Polly noticed something. The spider had a bright red-orange crest on its chest. Squinting into the shadows, she could make out the spider's two front legs, the tips of which were coloured dark red.

"Sor-Ben-Rez," breathed Polly.

"What, here?" whispered Marcia.

Polly nodded. "He's the spider!"

"But how do you...?"

Polly thrust out the Magic again, the giant spider scurrying back to the edge of darkness.

"G-o-o-o-o b-a-a-c-k," snarled the spider, its voice a series of rasping clicks.

"No!" said Polly firmly, being more brave than she'd ever been before in her entire life. "You're a nasty spider and you've been especially nasty to all the stick people. We've come to get the King back."

More clicking, this time filled with mocking laughter.

"Y-o-u-r s-t-u-p-i-d K-i-n-g i-s b-e-y-o-n-d

y-o-u-r r-e-a-c-h, l-i-t-t-l-e g-i-r-l. G-o b-a-c-k n-o-w, w-h-i-l-e y-o-u s-t-i-l-l h-a-v-e t-h-e c-h-a-n-c-e."

Marcia tugged from behind. "Maybe we should—"

Polly shrugged her off. "We're not going anywhere."

"F-o-o-l-i-s-h g-i-r-l," sneered the spider.
"Y-o-u h-a-v-e j-u-s-t s-e-a-l-e-d y-o-u-r f-a-t-e-!"

A web was forming at the edge of the light at an incredible speed, *thicker* and **thicker** and **thicker**, until the vanishing spider was lost from sight, his clicking words fading with him in the darkness.

"G-o-o-o-o b-a-a-c-k-!"

"Looks like we can't go any further," said Marcia, her voice tinged with relief.

"It's just a web," said Polly. "Just a bit thicker, that's all."

"It looks a lot thicker to me," said Marcia. "Maybe we should—"

"Marcia, do you really want to let the Queen down?"

Marcia shook her head, her blond curls like wobbling shadowy springs.

"Good, then that's settled," said Polly, sounding even more like her Mum than ever. "We're going to do this together or not at all."

"Do what?" asked Marcia, not sure she really wanted to know.

"Clear the web."

"Oh..."

Polly sighed. "It has to be the **two of us**, Marcia. Do you remember what the Queen said?"

Marcia nodded in the half-light.

"Then let's go."

The two friends scratched and scraped their way through the thick spidery web, ploughing through layer after layer after layer, the sticky strands clinging everywhere: arms, legs, hair and worst of all, their faces. After ages and ages the sea of webs came to an end. There in the distance was a faint portal of light.

An exhausted Polly rubbed off the sticky web strands, glad to be free from the clinging webs. Marcia, however, was still covered. Not only that, she was falling asleep.

"Marcia, wake up!"

Marcia yawned, her eyes already half-closed. *"Need to sleeeep..."*

Polly shook her friend, but it was no good; Marcia was falling into a deep sleep.

"Marcia, wake up! Wake up!" Polly shook harder, Marcia's web-encrusted curly hair a mass of webby candyfloss. "Marcia, please, please wake up!"

'Too many have already fallen asleep and been lost'

The sight of the dead stick men lying in a sea of webby strands flashed through Polly's mind.

The webs!

They were making Marcia fall into a deep sleep, and if she did...

Polly cleared away all the web strands covering the half-dozing Marcia as quickly as she could.

"Marcia, wake up! Wake up! You must wake up!"

Marcia's eyes flickered sleepily open. "P... Polly...?"

"Come on, Marcia. Come on, we have to go!"

"Go? Go where? So sleepy..."

"It's the webs. They're making you go sleepy, just like the stick men. We've got to get out of here. Look!" Polly pointed ahead. "It's the way out!"

"Way out?"

"Out of the webs and out of this horrible tree. Now, come on!"

Polly half dragged her friend who by now was thankfully coming back to life. By the time they got to the other end of the trunk, Marcia was web-less and fully awake.

"Polly, look at that!" she breathed, wide-eyed at the sight before them.

Chapter Eight

THROUGH THE SPIKES!

The trunk opening was suspended in mid-air with giant criss-crossing branches, some thick, some thin, stretching in all directions into the distance.

"Where now?" asked Marcia.

Polly studied their surroundings. Sticky strands of web were hanging down from the branches extending upwards, while the branches below remained clear.

"Up," she said.

"Up?" echoed Marcia, clearly not liking that idea. "I'm not very good at heights."

Polly unscrewed the top of the bubble container. "We'll use the Magic."

Moments later, the bubble hovered in the updraft invitingly. Polly went first, hopping through the bubble

57

wall and safely inside.

Marcia hesitated, the bubble bobbing just a step away.

"Come on, Marcia!"

Marcia gathered herself, the gap getting gradually wider as the bubble struggled to hold its position.

Polly reached impatiently through the bubble wall. "Take my hand."

Marcia hesitated, still unsure. The bubble wobbled against the updraft, inching further and further away.

"Marcia, I can't do this alone!"

Marcia took Polly's hand just as a strong gust broke the bubble free of its invisible moorings. Marcia screamed as she dangled helplessly. Polly couldn't hold on much longer. She reached through with her other hand.

"Stop struggling!"

Grabbing Marcia's flailing hand, Polly pulled with all her might, causing one of her feet to go straight through the bubble wall! Losing her balance, both girls tumbled backwards into the bubble, catapulting Marcia to safety.

'Five bubbles left,' whispered the disembodied voice as Polly pulled her trailing leg back through the bubble wall.

Up and up the bubble drifted through the maze of

criss-crossing branches, some as thick as small trees, others as thin as twigs, all of them crooked and loaded with spiky bubble-bursting potential.

There was no way they could dodge them all.

They were doomed to be

Quick as a flash, Polly was on her feet, dragging Marcia up with her. "We have to guide the bubble. Do as I do."

Polly began to shout directions...

"Run right!"

"Now left!"

"Marcia, quick, over here!"

"Now there!"

On and on, Polly carefully directed the magic bubble up through the spiky chaos looming overhead.

"This way, Marcia!"

"Quick, now here!"

"Over there!"

"Back over here!"

Navigating through the last of the treacherous branches, they were in the clear, almost...

Three very large branches drew together across the sky providing the only way through in a triangle of light far too small for their bubble to pass through.

The topside of the bubble wedged itself in the branchy triangle.

THEY WERE TRAPPED!

From the look on Marcia's face, it was clear that getting out and climbing through the remaining tree branches was not an option.

Maybe Polly could blow a smaller bubble...

'Five bubbles left...'

Polly put the container back in her pocket.

What now?

Polly had an idea. "Marcia, wait here."

"W… Where are you going?"

"I'm going to see if I can squeeze us through. If I can press on the outside of the bubble, I might just be able to squidge us through."

"I'm not sure…"

"Well, neither am I," said Polly, "but I can't think of anything else."

"What if the bubble pops?"

"Do you have any better ideas?" snapped Polly, her patience now stretched to its limit.

Marcia shook her head.

"In that case, I'm going outside. Wait here, and don't move unless I say."

Marcia nodded timidly.

Polly reached through the bubble and gripping hold of one of the branches, hauled herself up and out, until she was standing on the wooden limb. The updraft outside the bubble was billowing and strong.

"Be careful!" squeaked Marcia.

Polly reached over and pressed on the top of the bubble resting against one of the branches.

Her hand pushed straight through!

Oops! Too hard!

Polly tried again, this time much more gently. The springy surface of the bubble pushed in, but didn't break. With her other hand, she gently eased part of the bubble through the hole.

"It's working!" squealed Marcia, excitedly.

"Keep still," said Polly as she moved around to another branch and did the same again.

Then another branch...

another gentle press...

Bit by careful bit, the magic bubble squeezed itself through the hole, with Marcia hardly daring to move, the bubble now resembling a giant egg-timer.

With the bubble now almost through the triangle of branches, Polly climbed back inside to re-join Marcia.

"Now, if we reach through, we should be able to push ourselves free."

The two friends worked together, pushing this way and that, until eventually, the bubble floated free.

"Hurray!" cheered Marcia.

Their excitement was short-lived. Webby strands shot out of nowhere, sticking to the bubble and holding it fast. Thousands of tiny spiders scampered across the strands and onto the surface of the bubble.

Marcia shrieked. "Creepy-crawlies! Keep them away, keep them away!"

The bubble burst, sending both girls tumbling downwards onto the branches just below, Polly managing to grab Marcia just in time.

More webs, this time falling from above like nets.

There was no escape.

In a matter of seconds, *sleep washed over them...*

Chapter Nine

SOR-BEN-REZ

Polly opened her eyes, the smell of musty air filled her nostrils. There beside her was Marcia, still covered in webs and fast asleep. Polly tried to roll over, but her feet were stuck, tightly bound together by spider webs, anchored to the floor. She pulled again with all her strength, but the web held firm.

They were in a wooden chamber, which she guessed was part of the inside of one of the larger branches. The walls of the chamber were dark and patterned with strands of spider web, like an old house that had lain empty for too many years. There was something else, something just behind the hanging webs in the half-light. Polly shivered as stick men, many of them with their heads scattered on the floor like discarded footballs, stared lifelessly ahead.

Polly tugged in desperation at the webs around her feet, but they remained intact. She needed something she could use. Then she saw it, a stick, most probably a disembodied stick man arm, not far away.

Polly s−t−r−e−t−c−h−e−d, but the stick was just out of reach.

"Ah, awake I see," said a crackly voice.

One of the stick figures moved, coming alive from behind the thin veil of hanging webs. A taller stick man, half as big again as Izz and his brothers with a bright red-orange chest. Unblinking black pea eyes regarded her with amusement, a crooked smile spreading beneath his crookedy nose.

"Welcome to my home!" Sor-Ben-Rez said with a sweeping gesture of his stick arm.

"It's so nice of you to come and visit." Despite his smile, the tone of his voice suggested that he was far from pleased.

"What have you done with the King?" demanded Polly, her voice sounding a lot braver than she felt.

"The King is staying with me, as my special guest, until..." Sor-Ben-Rez's smile vanished. "I see you have brought the Magic."

Although Polly couldn't see its magical light, the Magic was clearly visible to Sor-Ben-Rez.

But why hadn't he taken it while she was asleep?

"Give it to me!" snapped the stick man.

"Where's the King?" asked Polly again, now feeling a little braver than before.

"Give me the Magic!" Sor-Ben-Rez's voice crackled like a bonfire of dry twigs.

"I want to see the King!" demanded Polly, holding her ground.

The former Royal Advisor shook with rage, the orangey-red on his chest blazing bright. "Why you insolent little cabbage, I can destroy you and your friend in an instant!" Sor-Ben-Rez's voice thundered around the chamber. Then he stopped and took a deep breath. When he spoke again, his voice was a low threatening whisper.

"Now, why don't you do something very sensible and give **the Magic** to me?"

Polly could feel herself shaking inside, her resolve starting to crumble. She didn't know what to do. What could she do? She was alone with no one to help.

"Give it to me!" Sor-Ben-Rez's anger boiled over.

"Now!"

Something inside Polly snapped. Without thinking, she shot out her hand. **The Magic** of the small container burst into life, blazing like a miniature sun, flooding the chamber with light and instantly vaporising all the webs caught in its glow.

Sor-Ben-Rez tumbled backwards, caught off-guard by this unexpected turn of events.

"Why don't you come and take it?" taunted Polly, the stick man's fear made her feel even more brave, though her hands were shaking. She stood up, her feet now free from the vaporised webs. A groan sounded from just behind; Marcia was beginning to stir.

"I WANT TO SEE THE KING!"

The light from **the Magic** intensified, as if fanned by the forcefulness of Polly's words. Fingers of light stretched into the far reaches of the wooden chamber, chasing away the shadows and darkness.

There, in the corner was a wooden cage, inside of which was the old man who had sold Polly the magic bubbles. Dejected and hunched on the floor with his knees drawn tight to his chest, his once sparkling blue eyes were dull and lifeless.

"Meet your precious King," rasped Sor-Ben-Rez. "The one you've come to rescue. Doesn't look much like a King now, does he?" he mocked, the cavern filling with laughter, not happy, smiley laughter, but the most horrible and crackly laughter imaginable.

Sor-Ben-Rez stepped closer. He had something in his hand; a hollow ball made of criss-cross strands. The ball started to glow **fiery red**, increasing in size as it burned **redder**

and

REDDER.

With a flick of his hand, Sor-Ben-Rez launched the **fire-stranded ball** straight at her.

The impact sent the bubble container flying from Polly's hand as she now floated inside the **fiery-webbed ball.**

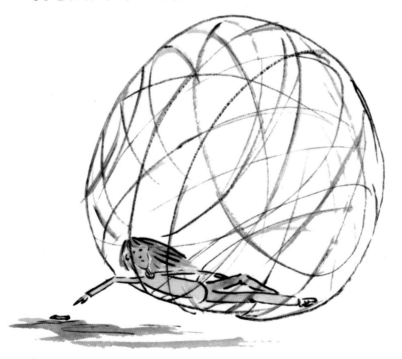

Polly lunged, trying to reach the bubble container on the floor, a lightning bolt of pain streaking up her arm as her hand brushed one of the red-webby strands.

Sor-Ben-Rez moved to collect his prize. Polly tried again, desperately reaching to retrieve the Magic, her fingers just inches short.

Polly s-t-r-e-t-c-h-e-d

and s-t-r-e-t-c-h-e-d.

Her fingers now almost touching...

The bubble container was snatched away by another webby ball, this one smaller and made up of

blue strands.

Sor-Ben-Rez gloated victorious. "Thank you, my dear. I will look forward to having both you and your precious King as my very special guests." He half-turned to leave before turning back again. "But now that I have the Magic..." Sor-Ben-Rez clenched his hand into a fist. The **fire-stranded ball** around Polly began to shrink.

"YOU BIG BULLY! LET ME GO! LET ME GO!"

Polly's screams were ignored.

Smaller and smaller and smaller...

The tightening **burning strands** were almost touching her...

Sor-Ben-Rez's laughter filled the chamber, the **blue-stranded** ball bobbing as it hovered alongside him. "I shall make sure that my spiderlings enjoy a great feast, if there's anything left of you to eat, that is."

Sor-Ben-Rez's laughter was unexpectedly cut short. The magic **blue-stranded** ball hurtled towards Polly as the stick man bent over in agony.

Blue and **Red** fireballs collided.

Both fireballs vanished in a blaze of light.

Polly was dumped on the floor, next to the magic bubble container.

"That's my best friend you're talking about," Marcia stepped out of the shadows, holding the stick that Polly had tried to reach earlier to free herself.

Sor-Ben-Rez staggered back to his feet. Moving his arms, another **red fireball** started to form.

Polly grabbed the magic container, unscrewing it as fast as she could.

The fully-formed **fireball** was growing rapidly. Taking a deep breath, Polly wasn't sure if she could blow the bubble in time, the tiny sphere growing

Bigger...

and BIGGER...

and BIGGER...

A frail voice echoed from behind. "One will not be enough. You will need the Power of Two."

Polly remembered the Queen's words:

'Two has great power.
Only two can rescue the King
and banish Sor-Ben-Rez forever.'

"MARCIA, QUICK, GET OVER HERE, I NEED YOU TO BLOW ANOTHER BUBBLE!"

Marcia hesitated. *"Can't you do it?"*

"IT TAKES TWO! Remember what the Queen said, 'TWO HAS GREAT POWER.' We need two to trap him! Blow inside my bubble."

Marcia dashed over to join Polly in the blowing, the second bubble now appearing inside the first one.

Bigger...
and BIGGER...
and **BIGGER...**

Twin bubbles and **fireball** both *grew in size*, but which one was going to be ready first?

Sor-Ben-Rez launched the **fireball** at the two girls. The double-skinned bubble bobbed as it finally detached itself from its tiny blower. The stick man grinned, instinctively knowing that he had won.

The **fireball** raced on a collision course with the bubble and the two hapless friends.

A BLAZE OF LIGHT ERUPTED!

Both **fireball** and bubble smashed into each other, with the **fireball** now becoming trapped inside the double-skinned bubble.

Changing course, the double-skinned bubble-fused **fireball** now accelerated rapidly towards a startled Sor-Ben-Rez.

The former Royal Advisor unable to avoid his fate, became trapped in the **fiery bubble** which promptly vanished through the walls of the chamber and into the world beyond.

Chapter Ten

SOME DIFFICULT CHOICES

"**W**ell done, well done!" came a voice from behind. "I knew you could do it! I knew you could do it!"

The old man was back. No longer weak and lifeless, but just as he was when Polly had first met him, blue eyes sparkling.

"I picked right! I picked right, and you did it! You really did it!"

The old man danced a celebration jig as Polly and Marcia looked on dumbfounded.

"How did you get out?" asked Polly. "You were trapped in a cage."

"What cage?"

"That cage..." Polly pointed to where the cage had been.

"Oh, that? It vanished when you defeated Sor-Ben-Rez. All part of his magic, you see." The old man danced another jig.

"So, you're the King then?"

The bubble seller beamed. "Indeed I am!"

"But, how could you sell me the bubbles when you were trapped here?"

"King magic," replied the King. "Not very powerful, but still very useful at times."

"You said you 'picked me'."

The King nodded.

"And me?" asked Marcia, "Did you pick me too?"

"Enough questions," the King's face turned very solemn. "You have some choices to make. Very difficult choices. Come, let us go outside."

Soon they were standing on a huge branch, high above the ground. The King took in the gloomy surroundings, his face downcast.

"The forest needs to be healed." The King sighed, suddenly looking very old indeed. "It will take Big Magic and the Power of Two."

"We can do it!" chirped Marcia.

The King looked at the curly headed girl and shook his head. "I'm afraid it's not you."

"But can't me and Marcia use the Power of Two again, like we did before?" asked Polly.

The King shook his head. "That's the wrong two."

"I don't understand," said Polly.

"The 'two' is you and me," said the King. "Marcia will have to go home." The King paused before continuing. "In order for **the Magic** to work, it has to be me and you. *That's why I chose you.*"

"Okay, so let's use **the Magic** first and then I'll go home with Marcia."

The King shook his head. "As I just said, I chose *you*. I chose you very carefully. It's time for Marcia to leave."

A sickening feeling swept through Polly giving her goose-bumps and sending chills through her body.

"There's only three bubbles left. If I use one for Marcia and two for the Big Magic, then..."

The King nodded. "There are difficult choices to be made."

"Can't you use someone else? What about one of the stick men, Izz maybe, or one of his brothers?"

"You hold the Magic. Only you can be part of the two." The King shook his head sadly. "Difficult choices."

"And the Big Magic will restore everything?" asked Polly.

The King nodded. "Just as it was before."

Polly gazed at the rusty brown forest stretching into the distance. "*This is too hard!* Why did you have to pick *me*?" Polly's stomach was doing sickly flip-flops.

Why did everything have to depend on her?

It was so unfair. Horrible, unthinkable decisions whirled round and round her mind in a tumble dryer of unfairness.

She couldn't take any more.

Polly took a deep breath. "I'm sorry, I have to go back."

The King's head dropped. "If that is your decision."

The sickness swelled inside her until it was almost unbearable. "I'm afraid it is. Come on, Marcia. It's time to go home."

Polly unscrewed the top of the small container and

blew. When the bubble was big enough, Marcia hopped inside.

"Come on, Polly, before I float away without you!"

"Goodbye, Marcia," said Polly.

"Eh? But you said you were coming back!"

"Yes, back with the King. Don't worry, it'll be all right. I'll come back as soon as I can."

The bubble started to drift off over the treetops, a helpless Marcia waving limply as she floated into the distance.

The King smiled sadly. "Thank you," he said. "Thank you, very much." He spread out his hands, taking in the whole forest. "As you can see, the poison is everywhere. We have to get back to the Tree of Light."

Polly took a deep breath, not really looking forward to the journey back, particularly as they had no more bubbles left to spare. She peered down at the branches criss-crossing into the depths towards the horrid Tree of Darkness.

The King smiled, but this time all sadness was gone. Cupping Polly's hands gently in his, he gave them a reassuring squeeze.

"Don't worry, I know a different way!" His eyes twinkled and somehow Polly knew that everything was going to be all right. "Hold tight, Polly, we're going on a journey!"

In the blink of an eye, they were inside the chamber again.

THEN SOMEWHERE ELSE...

THEN SOMEWHERE ELSE AGAIN...

AND AGAIN...

AND AGAIN...

travelling through murky chambers and passageways deep within the branches at impossible speeds.

Then it got dark.

VERY, VERY DARK.

The cold snapped at Polly's body, black teeth threatening to devour...

MORE CHAMBERS, FLASHING BY...

OVER...

AND OVER...

AND OVER...

Getting lighter... much lighter than before, although like the others, all were empty and unused.

THEN EVERYTHING

EXPLODED WITH LIGHT

Polly and the King were standing in the amphitheatre beneath the giant Tree of Light which arched high above them.

Polly was speechless.

The King beamed. "Being King has some advantages!" Bending close, his kindly face grew solemn. "Now, my dear, are you ready?"

Polly nodded, not really sure if she was ready or not.

"Now, picture what the forest used to look like."

Polly gazed at the depressingly rusty foliage and the bare earth.

"How can I? I don't know what it's supposed to look like."

The King smiled. "Close your eyes and take my hand." Polly followed the King's instructions. "Now, what do you see?"

Polly shook her head. "Nothing. I can't see *anything*!"

Polly searched the Darkness, but that's all there was. Darkness everywhere. She was about to open her eyes when something moved.

A shadow moved within the Darkness, becoming less and less shadowlike as it blossomed like a flower of green through the Dark. The forest started to appear all around her, no longer brown and withered, but lush and green and vibrant; the ground a carpet of fresh grass beneath her feet, with canopies of soft leaves above, and the air filled with the fragrance of wild spring flowers. Birds sang in the trees as red squirrels danced through the foliage.

The King's voice drifted on the breeze. "That's it, Pollyanna, let the life flow through you!"

Suddenly, **Polly was flying!**

Over the lush forest, then threading through the trees. Over streams and waterfalls.

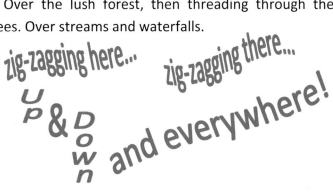

zig-zagging here... zig-zagging there... Up & Down and everywhere!

Polly had never felt so alive as new life flowed from her – it was the most fantastic feeling ever!

"Open your eyes, Polly, but keep seeing!"

Polly opened her eyes. The rusty brown of the foliage and the bare earth rushed in like a bleak tidal wave, bringing her down with a crash.

"Keep seeing!" urged the King. "Keep seeing!"

"I can't!" cried Polly. "It's all gone. It's all gone!"

The King was standing in front of her, filling her vision. "Only if you let it. Now, *see!*"

The lushness of the former forest flickered once more through her mind's eye, imposing itself over the dreary scene surrounding her.

"That's it!" said the King. "That's it! You're getting it! Now, stretch out your arms and dance!"

"But..."

"Dance, Pollyanna, Dance!"

And so she danced. Arms stretched wide, Polly whirled round and round. She felt lighter than air, as if she were flying through the forest again, with the birds singing and the squirrels scurrying.

"It's time to use the Magic," said the King.

Polly took out the small container and unscrewed the top. "I need your help to blow."

The King shook his head. "Just you."

"But... the Power of Two..."

The King looked at her earnestly. "The power is in you. Now, blow!"

Polly blew.

Slowly, the bubble began to form, getting

Bigger...

and BIGGER...

and BIGGER...

But this time it was different.

Inside the bubble, more bubbles were springing into life, thousands and thousands of tiny bubbles inside one huge bubble.

"The Magic is ready," said the King. "Release the bubbles."

Polly looked at the King, uncertain of what to do next. Then she knew.

She had to sing.

"I don't know if I can..."

The King squeezed her hand. "The Magic is inside you, Pollyanna. Open your mouth."

Polly opened her mouth and sang.

> She sang like she'd never sang before,
> singing words she'd never heard before,
> never known before.
> She sang and she sang and she sang,
> lost in the Magic.

POP!

The tiny bubbles streamed out into the forest. Everywhere a bubble touched suddenly burst to life as showers of rusty flakes fell away from the leaves to reveal lush green beneath.

THE FOREST WAS
COMING TO LIFE!

You have a song that only you can sing
A song that breathes life into everything'

Polly kept singing and singing, never wanting to stop. Life sprang up all around her: flowers budding and blooming in an instant; fresh green grass spearing through the mud, vivid pools of green growing

Larger and *Larger*

into great grassy lakes. It was the most wonderful sight ever as the image in her mind became a reality, as her song and thousands upon thousands of bubbles continued to work their restoring Magic.

Chapter Eleven

BY ROYAL APPOINTMENT

"Well done, well done!"

The King's voice cut through Polly's euphoria, ending both the song and the Magic. "You did it! You did it!"

Polly slumped to the ground, exhausted, her song like a fading dream.

Suddenly, she remembered. "It was you! The face in the bubble!"

The King nodded, a broad smile on his face and his eyes twinkling.

"But I don't understand, what about the Power of Two? I only blew one bubble."

The King crouched beside her. "I had to be sure of your heart. In order for the Big Magic to work, your heart needed to be for the stick people and the forest, first and foremost. That's why I chose you – I sensed your heart. And I was right!"

"But why didn't you tell me?"

"If I had told you, you would have had no decision to make."

"I don't understand."

"Your decision was the key. You sent Marcia away knowing that in doing so, you might never return yourself."

"So, you lied about the Power of Two just to keep me here," Polly was beginning to get flustered. "You tricked me!"

The King shook his head. "The Power of Two is real, but the two were you and—"

"Us!" The Queen walked into the clearing, resplendent in a dark emerald dress, her crown now a vibrant garland of fresh interwoven flowers.

"Your Majesty," the King bowed as the Queen approached. Behind her, an entourage of stick men, no longer unblinking and twig-like, but elf-like with fair complexions and eyes that were mesmerising and beautiful.

The Queen smiled. "We are one, the forest and all its folk, just as you are one. One and one makes two," she said as if that was enough, and it was.

Polly curtsied. "Forgive me, your Majesty."

The Queen smiled again, no longer a smile of regal restraint, but a dazzling smile that warmed the whole forest. "It is I who should ask your forgiveness, Pollyanna. For not making everything as clear as it might have been, but then..."

"I know," said Polly, not at all minding that the Queen had addressed her using her full name.

"As you can see," said the Queen, sweeping her arm in a flourish. "Everything has been restored and for that, we can never thank you enough." She tilted her head towards the King. "You chose well, my husband."

The King stepped forward and bowed, and taking the Queen's hand he kissed it tenderly. "It is good to see you again, Beloved."

The Queen caressed her husband's face lovingly. "As it is you, my Dearest."

Two wood elves stepped forward, carrying a long robe, which they fastened around the King's shoulders.

"Now, everything is as it should be," said the Queen. "The Poison is gone and Sor-Ben-Rez is no more." The Queen's gaze swept over the legions of gathered wood elves, who bowed in unison.

The Queen clapped her hands. "It's time for a celebration!"

Above them, the huge trunk of the Tree of Light was no longer in shadow and darkness. Instead, its intricate internal passages were transformed with the radiance of sparkling dancing lights as fairylike creatures weaved and danced, sprinkling showers of luminescent petals. As the floating petals touched the ground down, they magically transformed into all kinds of luscious fruit and berries: dark red plums, juicy strawberries, blackcurrants, blueberries, red and green grapes, tiny tomatoes, golden and red apples, cherries, peaches and lots of other fruit Polly had never seen before.

They all tucked into the delicious fruity feast, the cacophony of colours making Polly's mouth water. The flavours were as wondrous as the colours and textures. Earthenware goblets were passed around brimming with golden liquid, the sweetness of which Polly had never tasted before, and no matter how much of the delicious juice she drank, her goblet magically remained full to the brim. The wood elves danced and sang, playing leaf-gilded instruments and pipes as everybody ate and drank their fill. As the fruit feast was devoured, more and more sparkling petals descended, transforming into heaps and heaps of delicious fruit.

At the height of the celebrations, the Queen clapped her hands. The music faded and the forest became still.

"A position has recently become available. A position of great responsibility. A position trusted to only a few through the ages." She paused to take in her subjects. "The position of Head Counsel and Royal Advisor is now to be granted. Would those of suitable rank make themselves known?"

Polly looked on in fascination as the elf crowds hustled and bustled amongst themselves, wondering which ones were to step forward.

After several minutes, all the murmurings and jostling died down, but no one had stepped forward.

The King whispered into the Queen's ear. The Queen nodded and addressed the crowd again. "As no one considers themselves suitable for this noble task, we will make the decision ourselves."

There was a hushed silence as the Queen swept her royal gaze over her subjects.

"The decision has been made."

More hushed silence.

"The position of Head Counsel and Royal Advisor is to be bestowed upon..."

The air of expectation rose to new heights.

"Miss Pollyanna."

There was a brief silence before the whole forest erupted into spontaneous cheers and chants of

Pollyanna! Pollyanna!

filling the whole assembly.

Polly was stunned.

How could she counsel anyone? She was only a young girl who had enough difficulty making decisions for herself, let alone Stick Royalty. She was about to protest when the Queen spoke again.

"Pollyanna, as our honoured guest and in celebration of your new position, we would also like to grant you one wish." The Queen leant close to address Polly privately. "Whatever you wish that is in my power to give, my dear, it shall be granted."

Polly had never been granted a wish before. Having a wish was something that she and her friends had all thought about at one time or another, but now, she actually had one!

A real wish.

A single wish.

What would she wish for?

What *could* she wish for?

Glancing at the Queen and King and the gathered multitudes, Polly knew that she could have anything she wanted.

Anything in the whole world.

Her mind raced.

What could it be?

What should it be?

The weight of expectation grew as they awaited the new Head Counsel and Royal Advisor's reply. The more Polly thought, the harder it became, until her head became a mindless spaghetti of possibilities, far too many to choose from.

Then, suddenly, she knew...

Polly stood up and cleared her throat. "Thank you, your Majesties. I feel very honoured that you should choose me as your new Head Counsel and Royal Advisor."

More cheers rang out and floated to the tree tops.

"But I fear that it is not a position that I can accept."

Gasps of incredulity and disappointment swept through the crowd.

"So, as my first and last advice to Your Majesties, I would bestow this incredible position on not one, but four people, so that what has happened before may never happen again."

The forest hushed to deathly silent, apart from a few muted whispers.

Polly motioned to the four brothers. "Izz, Ozz, Igg and Ogg, please step forward."

The four brothers jostled their way to the front, no longer a scraggly collection of sticks and twigs, but four handsome young elf men.

The Queen turned to address Polly privately. "Is this really your wish, dear?"

Polly nodded.

The Queen smiled as she turned to address the crowds. "So be it. Henceforth, Izz, Ozz, Igg and Ogg will be our Head Counsel and Royal Advisors!"

The four brothers bowed low as four glimmering cloaks were brought forward and adorned on the siblings, one red, one green, one blue and one yellow. The forest erupted into cheers and loud applause as the names of the four brothers filled the twilight.

Polly turned to the Queen. "Your Majesty, I do have one bubble left, and if it pleases you, I would like to go home."

The Queen smiled. "It pleases me very much, though it is a great shame," her smile faded. "You would have made a very wise Head Counsel and Royal Advisor."

A space was quickly cleared as Polly prepared to leave.

"What about Marcia?" asked Polly.

Marcia was terrible at keeping secrets and would be eager to tell anyone and everyone all about their adventures with in the magical land of Dizzelwood.

The King smiled enigmatically. "Don't worry, young Marcia will think it all a dream." He dabbed his nose with a royal finger. "Let's keep it our little secret."

"Thank you, your Majesty," Polly took out the small container, unscrewing the cap for one last time.

Just one bubble left.

In no time at all, the bubble grew large enough and was waiting to depart.

"How will I get home?"

"The bubble knows the way," said the King. "Thank you for everything."

As Polly was about to enter the bubble, the four new Royal Advisors stepped forward, bowing low.

"Thank you from us too," said Izz, looking splendid in his red robes. "We shall endeavour to live up to your trust."

Polly smiled, giving each a big hug. "I'm sure you will!"

As soon as she was inside, the bubble left floated steadily upwards, amid deafening cheers and applause.

Pollyanna! Pollyanna!

Polly waved, tears in her eyes and sad to be leaving, but also glad to be going home.

What would she tell her parents?

Polly would never forget her incredible adventure.

Never.

As the bubble rose high above the tree canopy into the fading light, she couldn't help noticing how different the forest looked, how vibrant and alive!

With those happy thoughts ringing in her ears, Polly

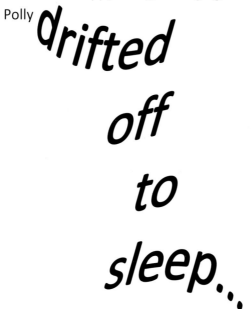

drifted off to sleep...

Chapter Twelve

A STRANGE MESSAGE

"**L**ook, do you want this or not? It's the last one," the Bubble gun seller fidgeted, clearly in a rush to make his final sale and go home.

Polly looked at the £2.50 in her hand.

"Why don't you sell it to one of the other children," said a voice. An old man was standing next to Polly beaming brightly. "I'm sure we can find something much better for her to spend all her hard-earned pocket money on!"

Polly stared at the old man in his crumpled jacket. "I'm sorry, do I know you?"

Something clicked into place: a distant dream, a memory, or maybe a bit of both.

Polly almost screamed, wide-eyed. "IT'S YOU!"

"Come, dear," he said, leading her away.

"I... I thought it was a dream, I mean, something I imagined."

The old man's eyes twinkled. "I have something for you. Something that I want you to look after. Something very special."

"POLLYANNA!"

Polly nearly jumped out of her skin.

"What *are* you doing?" her Mum was marching towards her.

The old man was gone.

Polly was in **BIG TROUBLE.**

"Sorry, Mum. I was... er..." Polly thought she'd better not say anymore; she shouldn't be talking to strangers, even those she thought she might have known, in a strange sort of way.

"Come on," said Mum, "it looks like it's going to rain."

Polly sighed, all thoughts of the strange old man now gone completely.

Why did it always rain on school holidays?

Re-joining her Dad and two brothers, they quickly made their way back home.

Back in her bedroom, Polly pottered about as the rain pattered against the window. She fished in her pocket for the £2.50 to put back in her money box.

Her money was gone, and her pockets empty.

No, not empty.

She pulled out a piece of yellowed paper wrapped tightly around a small green container with a shiny gold top that shone like the sun.

Carefully unravelling the paper, she read the scrawled note inside:

Thank you for purchasing your Magic Bubbles!
To be used only in Emergencies.
KEEP VERY, VERY SAFE
Hopefully see you soon!

What a strange message!

What could it mean?

Sunlight burst through the window. The shower had passed.

There was a knock on the door.

"It's Marcia!" shouted her Mum from downstairs. "Come on down, I've just made some sandwiches."

Polly wrapped the little container back in the yellowed paper and put it on her bookshelf where perhaps she could look at it later. It would be good to see Marcia. Now that the sun was out, perhaps they could go on a little adventure!

If you enjoyed this adventure,
why not drop us a line at
www.tomsercat.com/write-book-review
and we will publish your review
on our website for others to read!

Join Polly on her next fantastic adventure!

Spiders! Spiders! Spiders!

Dad's precious pipe has gone missing...
Marcia's lost her voice!
Spiders are rampaging everywhere!
Not only that, Polly's family are trapped like statues beneath giant spider webs!

Polly, along with her bookworm big brother, Jake, and best friend, Marcia, set out to stop the evil Sor-Ben-Rez and his spider army from taking over the world!

Armed with just a bottle of Magic Bubbles and their wits, can the intrepid companions discover and unlock the mysterious Power of Three?

Will Jake prove a hindrance or a help to their mission?

Will Sor-Ben-Rez capture the Magic Bubbles and use them in his dastardly plans for world domination?

200 pages of full colour high adventure!
Available only from Tomser Cat Books
www.tomsercat.com

Something Very Strange...

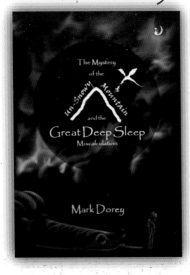

Snow never, *Ever* settled on

Rudry Mountain

Some said it was

Magic

or perhaps the

Mountain

was made of

Hot Rock

but the Truth lay somewhere in between...

What's more, lots of fresh fruit has been mysteriously vanishing from the greenhouses of Rudry village...

Tyler and his Grandpa set out on an unexpected adventure to unravel the secrets of the Mountain and so much more!

160 pages of full colour high adventure!
This book is 2 books in 1!
Look inside for

A Brief History of Dragons!